Three Talks and a Few Words

Three Talks and a Few Words at a Festive Occasion

Talks by
RICHARD USBORNE
on Thursday, 8 April 1982
WILLIAM DOUGLAS-HOME
on Tuesday, 13 April 1982
MALCOLM MUGGERIDGE
on Wednesday, 28 April 1982 at the
Lyttelton Theatre
and an address given by
ANGUS MACINTYRE
on Tuesday, 6 April 1982 at
Strand House

LONDON
1983

ISBN 0-87008-103-9

Published by James H. Heineman, Inc.
475 Park Avenue
New York, NY 10022

H

Permission to quote graciously granted
by Edward Cazalet

The first edition was printed by
The Curwen Press, London, England
Second printing 1991 by BookCrafters,
Chelsea, Michigan

The first edition was limited to 500 copies

This is Number 4 of a series
of monographs on P.G. Wodehouse
Series ISSN 0734-2683

Number 1,
Dr Sir Pelham Wodehouse Old Boy
by Richard Usborne
was published in 1978
The first 100 were numbered
ISBN 0-87008-100-4

Number 2,
P.G. Wodehouse 1881-1981
by Frances Donaldson
and Richard Usborne
was published in 1982
The first 100 were numbered
ISBN 087008-101-2

Number 3,
The Toad at Harrow
P.G. Wodehouse in Perspective
by Charles E. Gould, Jr
was published in 1982
The first 100 were numbered
ISBN 087008-102-0

INTRODUCTION

For two months, mid-March to mid-May, of 1982 there was an Exhibition, P. G. WODEHOUSE: A CENTENARY CELEBRATION, in the foyers of the National Theatre on the South Bank of London's river. Manuscripts, letters, pictures, first editions, originals of illustrations of Wodehouse stories in English and American magazines . . . memorabilia of all sorts. And Madame Tussaud's lent their own life-size image of the relaxed author, sitting, in an open-neck, short-sleeve shirt, spectacles on nose, pipe in hand. (Twice, during the run of the Exhibition, acquisitive visitors tried unsuccessfully to get away with the pipe: each time breaking a waxen finger.)

About two evenings a week there were speakers on the stage of the Lyttelton Theatre, giving talks on Wodehousian subjects. Here, for the record, are three of the talks, and an after-dinner speech on the occasion when Queen Elizabeth, the Queen Mother, not least of Wodehouse fans, was the guest of Mrs Simon Hornby. Sheran Hornby, *née* Cazalet, is Lady Wodehouse's granddaughter. Lady Wodehouse, then aged ninety-six if a day, sent a 'Wish Plummie and I could be with you' message from Long Island. Plummie would have been a hundred and one. But he died seven years short of his century: Sir Pelham Wodehouse, Knight of the British Empire and Honorary D.Litt. of Oxford.

SOME RECENT WODEHOUSE SCHOLARSHIP

Richard Usborne

at the Lyttelton Theatre, 8 April 1982

'Cats are not dogs!'

There is only one place where you can hear good things like that thrown off quite casually in the general run of conversation, and that is the bar parlour of the Anglers' Rest. Although the talk up to this point had been dealing with Einstein's Theory of Relativity, we readily adjusted our minds to cope with the new topic. In our little circle I have known an argument on the Final Destination of the Soul to change inside forty seconds into one concerning the best method of preserving the juiciness of bacon fat.

That's the opening of one of the Mulliner stories, as you may have recognized. In the next half-hour or so you will find me, too, changing my subjects, unpardonably often. I chose the title of this talk . . . Wodehouse Scholarship . . . long before I got down to preparing it. You must stand by for incoherence on a massive scale.

But I have it in mind mainly to talk about three recent books. One is *Thank You, Wodehouse* . . . by two Oxford dons, Doctors J. H. C. Morris and A. D. Macintyre, both of Magdalen. My second, *In Search of Blandings*, is by a serving Army officer, Colonel Norman Murphy. I believe he is, to my embarrassment, in the audience out there. I have been afraid of colonels from the days when I was an awkward squaddie in the ranks of my school Officers' Training Corps, but I shall be frank and fearless about this excellent book. My third book is *Wodehouse at War*, by Iain Sproat, Member of Parliament and now a Junior Minister in Mrs Thatcher's team. I would sooner not incur the wrath of a Junior Minister, either, but here again I shall be upright, downright and straightforward.

These three books represent three main avenues of what I am pompously calling Wodehouse Scholarship.

1. The first avenue: with seeming innocence you take Wodehouse's fiction as fact, his characters as real people, and you assume that he never made any mistakes. This gets you into a lot of lovely problems, most often about dates,

and you spend a lot of lovely time solving them, and teasing other critics who have either not tackled these problems or have not found the right answers to them. This makes a number of pleasant essays, and this is the method of those Oxford dons in their pleasant book *Thank You, Wodehouse.*

2. The second avenue: you accept Wodehouse's fiction as fiction, but you suspect that there is a lot of fact behind it, and you go after pairings . . . fiction based on fact. That's Colonel Murphy's method in *In Search of Blandings.*

3. The third avenue is purely biographical/factual, as in Iain Sproat's book, *Wodehouse at War.* Now that the Home Office has at last taken the wartime documents out from under wraps, Sproat spreads them on the desk and examines them, to learn just what did happen to poor Wodehouse in the 1940–1944 wartime period, why did he make those five Talks to America from Berlin (even the benign *New Yorker,* and only recently, referred to them as 'infamous'), what did the world say and . . . most important, why the hell did the Home Office keep it all under wraps for thirty-seven years? The result, of course, is a belated vindication of Wodehouse. He had been an ass but not a villain. And he suffered for it much more than he deserved, or ever let on.

In *Thank You, Wodehouse* the don authors ask themselves such questions as: What was Bertie's age? How many uncles had he? At which Oxford college was he an undergraduate? (He says, himself, that he was at Magdalen, and surely he should know. But how come he rode a bicycle round the fountain in the nude after a bump supper? Magdalen doesn't have a fountain.) How many girls had Bertie kissed when last heard of? To how many was he engaged on and off? (Remember, he was engaged for several days to Pauline Stoker in New York and he states specifically that he didn't kiss her, for various reasons . . . a cold in the head and the arrival of the waiter with the beef sandwiches.) What was the chronology of the Blandings stories . . . which follows which and at how long a distance of real time? *Was* Ronnie the *il*legitimate son of General Sir Miles Fish and Lord Emsworth's sister Julia? With how many sisters was Lord Emsworth cursed? How many secretaries? How many pig-minders? How many calories per day did Lord Emsworth's prize pig, Empress of Blandings, consume in her diet? Where was Market Blandings? And what about the train service to and from Paddington? All these questions and many more...

Colonel Murphy's *In Search of Blandings* is not by any means all about Blandings. Its sub-title, 'The Facts Behind the Wodehouse Fiction', gives a truer description of its contents. Murphy goes deeply into Shropshire and the Threepwood clan. But he also noses round Norfolk, Sussex, Mayfair, Wimbledon and Emsworth (which is in Hampshire), playing a game of Snap when a fictional place or person in the books echoes a real place or person in Wodehouse's own life. Murphy combs through the Wodehouse entries in *Burke* and *Debrett*, through Post Office Guides, through parish registers of births and deaths. At Somerset House he dug out the names, addresses and wills of more than fifty of Plum Wodehouse's cousins and other relatives.

The name Wodehouse, as you may know, goes back deep into history in Norfolk. There is no mention of a Wodehouse to tie in with the Wooster whom Bertie's Aunt Dahlia mentions . . . the one who would, in the Crusades, have captured Joppa single-handed if he hadn't fallen off his horse. But there was an interesting nineteenth-century worthy, John Wodehouse, first Earl of Kimberley, 1826–1902. I've been looking him up in the *Dictionary of National Biography*. He had been British Minister at St Petersburg, Lord Lieutenant of Ireland (we note that, as such, he reported, in November 1865, 'the heart of the people is against us, and I see no prospect of any improvement within any time that can be calculated'). He became Secretary for the Colonies, and for his earldom chose the title of Kimberley . . . a village near his birthplace in Norfolk. I quote again from the *DNB* 'When the British flag was hoisted in the diamond fields, the township was called Kimberley after the Colonial Secretary'. Lord Kimberley became Foreign Secretary and a Knight of the Garter. His third son married a daughter of Matthew Arnold. John Wodehouse, first Earl of Kimberley was, as far as I can work it out, Plum Wodehouse's great-uncle.

In his search for Blandings Castle, Murphy finds a useful starting-point in Stableford, a town in Shropshire where, we know, Wodehouse's parents took a house, and where Plum came from Dulwich for school holidays. But Murphy also keeps a wary eye on Cheltenham, where young Wodehouse also spent some school holidays. What stately homes round these parts might have given him a shape for Blandings later, and a railway system similar to the one he postulates between Market Blandings and Paddington? I am revealing no secrets when I say that he makes a strong case for Sudeley Castle in Gloucestershire being the fictional Blandings Castle for its architecture and railway system, and Weston Park being Blandings Castle for its estate and gardens, with the village of Weston-Under-Lizard as the probable Blandings Parva.

In the context of Blandings Castle, where is it? what was it?, I want to slip in here a small contribution of my own. It is a vexed subject . . . what was the layout of rooms, the inner structure of the castle? Where were the dining-rooms, the billiard-room, the Portrait Gallery, Lord Emsworth's study? Wodehouse gives a number of conflicting pointers, but I have made this discovery. . . . It is now known to Wodehouse scholars as the UCCWC . . . the Usborne Caveat of Confusion Worse Confounded. Briefly, it is that Wodehouse flitted carelessly between the English and American ways of describing floor-levels of a house. An American might say that the great front door of the castle opened on to the ground floor *or* the first floor . . . but the floor above is to him always the second floor. We in England say the first floor up is the first floor. Wodehouse writes it both ways, to the confusion of architects and anybody else who's trying to map out the geography of the castle. You've got to watch it carefully.

In many directions of research, other than in looking for Blandings, Murphy is able to claim 'Obviously Wodehouse was thinking of factual X when he wrote fictional Y'. A small example: in his first grown-up novel, *Love Among the Chickens*, 1906, there is a handyman named Beale, ex-Army. Murphy discovers that the Sergeant-Major in charge of the Officers' Training Corps at Dulwich in Wodehouse's time as a boy was named Beale. And I'll be telling you later, thanks to Colonel Murphy, about Wodehouse's cousin, Helen Marion Wodehouse, Mistress of Girton College, Cambridge, from 1931 to 1942.

Fiction combed for fact, fact for illuminations on fiction. Murphy is specially good on the 'Pink 'Un' and Pelican Club background for Galahad's raffish youth and friends.

Iain Sproat's book, as I say, is all fact, no fiction. I nominate it as scholarship for the way Sproat went after his facts, picking locks and breaking down doors to get them. As you know, the Wodehouses at the beginning of the war, 1939, were living in their house – their only home – in Le Touquet in northern France. They were there when the German armies swept west in 1940, and Wodehouse, as a male enemy alien under the age of sixty . . . he was nearly fifty-nine . . . soon had to go off to civilian internment. He found himself released a few months before his sixtieth birthday and was brought to Berlin, where he accepted the invitation of a chap in the German Foreign Office, whom he had known in Hollywood, to record five Talks to America for the radio . . . America was not yet in the war.

The talks were cheerful, funny, completely Wodehousian . . . about his experiences, in various uncomfortable railway-trucks, and prisons, and barracks, and camps, on his way to the last camp, a converted lunatic asylum. Innocent though the Talks were, it goes without saying that, as a British citizen in wartime, he should *NOT* have accepted the invitation to speak on the German radio. There was an immediate outcry against him in England and a good deal of disapproval in America. He never came back to England after the war and the cloud under which his name lay took a long time to disperse, largely because the official papers on the matter were not released to the public. Thirty-four years later and forty-five days before he died, at the age of ninety-three, Wodehouse was given a Knighthood. But the papers on his interrogation in Paris after its Liberation in 1944 . . . these were still kept under wraps. It made people feel that, in spite of the Knighthood, there must have been *some*thing that the authorities wanted to keep secret. . . .

Iain Sproat, among others, had been trying to get the Home Office to unbelt the papers, or give the reason why not. And eventually, only last year, the Home Office did unbelt them, and Iain Sproat was the first to see them. Sproat gives the whole story . . . a diary of the events themselves, the documents, the five Talks *verbatim*, the interrogation, the questions in Parliament and so on. You must read it, and not least the Home Office's strange reasons for not having let us have chapter and verse till after Wodehouse's death. There are still certain gaps, I think, in the story, but none, I am sure, that will, when filled in, tarnish the Wodehouse record as it now stands. And no doubt Frances Donaldson's official *Life* of Wodehouse, due to be published this autumn, and based on family papers and much else new, will fill the gaps in. But the Sproat book, the Sproat scholarship, has done a fine job, for us, and for poor Wodehouse. And a curse on the faceless bureaucracy which kept a good man's reputation under a cloud for thirty-four unnecessary years!

I'd like to boast now of an item of fortuitous scholarship that I claim to have contributed to the stockpile. It came my way by luck, and it was new to Wodehouse himself. It's a small point, and, if you are an admirer of the father of Christopher Robin and author of *Winnie the Pooh* and that lot, you must close your ears. In July 1941 the *Daily Telegraph*'s correspondence columns were filled with letters cursing Wodehouse – for being a traitor, an imbecile and, indeed, a no-good writer . . . also a disgrace to Oxford which had given him an Honorary Doctorate of Letters just before the war.

Almost the first of these letters heaving bricks at Wodehouse in the *Telegraph* was one from A. A. Milne. I think Milne would have agreed with Confucius' statement 'There is no spectacle more agreeable than to observe an old friend fall from a roof-top'. His letter . . . you'll find it in full in Sproat's book . . . was bland, subtle and damaging. He said, in effect, 'Poor, silly Plum, he's escaped again. He ought to have fought in the 1914 war, but he stayed in America and didn't. He ought to have paid his Income Taxes between the wars, but he didn't. And now, for the sake of a comfortable suite in the Adlon Hotel in Berlin, he is giving weekly talks on the German radio. He has escaped again. . . .'

The Milne letter continues:

> I remember that he told me once that he wished he had a son; and he added characteristically (and quite sincerely): 'But he would have to be born at the age of fifteen, when he was just getting into his House eleven.' You see the advantage of that. Bringing up a son throws a considerable responsibility on a man; but by the time the boy is fifteen one

> has shifted the responsibility on to the housemaster, without forfeiting any reflected glory that may be about. This, I felt, had always been Wodehouse's attitude to life. . . . But . . . irresponsibility in what the papers call a 'licensed humorist' can be carried too far: naïveté can be carried too far. Wodehouse has been given a good deal of licence in the past, but I fancy that now his licence will be withdrawn. . . .

I had been in the Middle East at the time of the Wodehouse Berlin broadcasts. It wasn't till I found myself involved, in the late 1950s, in writing a book about Wodehouse's books, that I set myself to catch up on them, reading and re-reading and, in a number of Saturday visits to the British Library newspaper archive at Colindale, to see what all the 1941 papers had said about the broadcasts, and why all the fuss. I happened to be reading *Psmith in the City* (date 1910) when Milne's letter to the *Telegraph* was fresh in my mind. In that early novel I found young Mike Jackson, Psmith's friend, voicing . . . or rather, having the narrator voice for him . . . an opinion in print significantly similar to that imputed to Wodehouse himself in alleged conversation with Milne. Listen to this:

> Mike got on with small girls reasonably well. He preferred them at a distance, but, if cornered by them, could put up a fairly good show. Small boys, however, filled him with a sort of frozen horror. It was his view that a boy should not be exhibited publicly until he reached an age when he might be in the running for some sort of colours at a public school.

I wrote to Wodehouse about this, thinking he might just possibly not have spotted the echo. He hadn't. He told me Milne hadn't really been a friend of his, and he certainly had never said that, or anything like it, to Milne. But the imputed remark *had* rung a distant bell for him, and now I had located its source.

I'm glad to say that Compton Mackenzie had been infuriated by Milne's letter in the *Telegraph*, and he wrote the Editor a snorter . . . 'a disgrace that the man who had made such a good thing out of his own son as Milne, should have attacked Wodehouse that way . . . '. Alas, the *Telegraph* didn't print Mackenzie's letter. But it's in his many-volumed *Memoirs*.

Goodness, how sad the whole of that story of the Berlin broadcasts was! Wodehouse, in his post-war novels, did make pinprick teases of some of the people who spoke out against him in 1941. Gussie Fink-Nottle, you remember, up before the beak for newt-hunting after midnight in a Trafalgar Square fountain, gave his name as Alfred Duff Cooper.... It was Duff Cooper who, as Minister of Information, had got Cassandra of the *Daily Mirror* ... William (later Sir William) Connor ... to spit that vile philippic against Wodehouse on the BBC radio ... let it be said that the BBC was all against it, but the Minister overrode them. And A. A. Milne again ... there are two or three good teases of the Christopher Robin stuff in the Wodehouse golf stories. And in *The Mating Season* Bertie Wooster gets orders to recite Christopher Robin verses at a village concert, and his agony is terrible.

But – still on Milne – I commend to you also a half page of typescript in an upright glass-case in this Exhibition ... the case on the right as you stand with your back to the windows on the second floor. It was a stray page found in Wodehouse's study at home after his death. It is something he had typed, and then crossed out in pencil ... and he had used the paper to type something on the other side. But the half page he had typed and crossed out is an expert sleeve across the Milne windpipe. I don't know what it was for ... something to be published in his memoirs? For a book to be called *Over Ninety?* Anyway, Wodehouse seems to have decided that he couldn't use it ... perhaps that it was out of character for him to show that he had minded Milne hitting him below the belt during the war ... out of character to be giving Milne the chop in reply. But I am delighted that this stray half page of Wodehouse typescript should have been rescued, and its words made available to posterity:

> Milne is the author of *Winnie-the-Pooh* and other works, and I have known him off and on for nearly forty years. He has never been a very popular man for one reason and another, and it was in the hope of giving him a rather wider circle of admirers that I once founded the Try To Like Milne Club. It never really caught on. After a great deal of canvassing I could find only one man who was willing to join, and he wrote me a week later saying 'I'm sorry. I shall have to resign from the Try To Like Milne Club. I've just met him.'

The book, by the Oxford dons, *Thank You, Wodehouse*, puts Wodehouse among those much-loved authors with whose works saints and scholars relax when they know they ought to be reading their bibles, or studying the works of Sophocles or Spinoza . . . the Sherlock Holmes stories, *Alice in Wonderland*, Stevenson's *The Wrong Box*, some Shakespeare and Trollope's Barsetshire. These saints and scholars produce specialist spoof scholarship as a 'displacement activity' . . . what they hope will be taken as a justification for their laughing in an armchair when they should be at their desks surrounded by dictionaries, commentaries, concordances and things, like . . . to use a Wodehouse image . . . like sea-beasts among rocks. Whatever their consciences may say, they are paying tribute to their beloved authors by giving their stuff the donnish treatment as though it were the Bible, Sophocles or Spinoza.

I don't say I know of any dons or divines whose displacement activities has been quite so time-consuming as those of a certain Bishop of Wells of the not too distant past. He is reported to have said 'I like to get my golf over in the mornings so that I can have the afternoons for bridge'. I wonder how he relaxed in the evenings. He was of too early a date to have been tempted by the works of Wodehouse.

I suppose the grave of Conan Doyle, with the Sherlock Holmes stories, has come in for the most frequent and continuous laying on of such wreaths and bouquets by amateur and professional scholars. I possess those two monster and expensive volumes entitled *The Annotated Sherlock Holmes*, containing all the stories, all the *Strand Magazine* illustrations, and acres and acres of solemn notes and essaylets such as Sherlock Holmes addicts exchange in their magazines, and at their dinners and club meetings. I read the other day, didn't I, that the Abbey National people in Baker Street, whose building might be said to stand where Number 221A stood, get . . . wasn't it? . . . some two thousand letters a year . . . or was it a week? . . . or a day . . . addressed either direct to Mr Sherlock Holmes or to Abbey National for passing on . . . and they are all courteously answered, presumably by some Sherlock Holmes scholar. I remember that on the one occasion when I visited the Wodehouses in their home on Long Island, I was shown into Plum's study, first by his wife Ethel . . . perhaps Plum was getting the drinks out. On his desk in the study was a big, neatly stacked, basket of letters, mostly in air-mail envelopes. Ethel Wodehouse said, with an expression of wifely disapproval, 'Plummie insists on answering every letter. I wish he wouldn't'. Later I was in the study with Plum himself and he pointed to the letter tray and said, a little sadly, 'Ethel insists on my answering all the letters I get'.

I think the style of such spoof examinations of favourite books of entertainment is based on the plodding German scholarship of the early nineteenth century, when German pundits got into the Bible, the Greek and Latin classics and Shakespeare. I'm sure it is great fun, for the addict, to write in this style of spoof solemnity. The master of it . . . or, say, the man whose publications of such literary displacement activities I know best and have enjoyed most . . . is Monsignor Ronald Knox. He was a man of deep and reverent Catholic faith, of great industry and of restless brilliance, ingenuity and humour who, for relaxation, set himself awful problems of rhyme and reason for the pleasure of working them out, in English, Latin, Greek or (latterly) Hebrew . . . the more difficult the better.

Knox was one of the numerous dons and divines . . . he was both in his time . . . who read Wodehouse regularly and with great admiration. I wish he had included Wodehouse among his subjects for extramural publication. He was one of the first, perhaps *the* first, to apply this kind of scholarship to Sherlock Holmes . . . he clearly knew the stories backwards. There is a long essay in his book, *Essays in Satire*, entitled 'Studies in the literature of Sherlock Holmes'. He later goes on to study similarly Trollope's Barsetshire novels, Bunyan's *Pilgrim's Progress*, Boswell's *Life of Johnson* and, in the manner of Freudian psycho-analysis, the Struwwelpeter verses. For good measure he also proves, in imitation and mockery of the methods of those who prove, by cyphers, that Bacon, or a number of other people, wrote Shakespeare . . . Knox proves, by cyphers, that Queen Victoria wrote Tennyson's 'In Memoriam' . . . I say Tennyson's, but that's wrong. The cyphers show that Queen Victoria wrote it, and used Tennyson as a front man, just as Bacon had used Shakespeare.

Well, I'd like to read you a bit of Knox's introduction to his Sherlock Holmes essay, because it exactly defines the approach of these Oxford dons to Wodehouse's works:

> If there is anything pleasant in life, it is doing what we are not meant to do. If there is anything pleasant in criticism, it is finding out what we are

> not meant to find out. It is the method by which we treat as significant what the author did not mean to be significant, by which we single out as essential what the author regarded as incidental. Thus, if one brings out a book on turnips, the modern scholar tries to discover from it whether the author was on good terms with his wife; if a poet writes on buttercups, every word he says may be used as evidence against him at an inquest of his views on a future existence. On this fascinating principle, we delight to extort economic evidence from Aristophanes, because Aristophanes knew nothing of economics: we try to extract cryptograms from Shakespeare, because we are inwardly certain that Shakespeare never put them there: we sift and winnow the Gospel of St Luke, in order to produce a Synoptic problem, because St Luke, poor man, never knew the Synoptic problem to exist.
>
> There is, however, a special fascination in applying this method to Sherlock Holmes, because it is, in a sense, Holmes's own method. 'It has long been an axiom of mine,' he says, 'that the little things are infinitely the most important....'

Then Knox goes on for thirty scholarly pages about why Dr John Watson's wife calls him James, about whether Holmes had been at Oxford or Cambridge and for how long, about the probable *two* Sherlock Holmeses, and the alleged death of one of them grappling with Moriarty on the Reichenbach Falls, about how a pencil marked with the maker's name, Johann Faber . . . two n's at the end of Johann . . . could be worn down to a stump with only the two n's left on it – about the dating of the stories – a comparison of a moment in 'The Speckled Band' with a moment in Aeschylus's *Agamemnon* play . . . and so on . . . lovely, loving donnish stuff . . . the don at ease and at play.

I think that these essays of Knox were mostly, if not all, papers that he had prepared for the literary and convivial paper-reading societies which proliferate in public schools and universities (he had been a Scholar at Eton, an undergraduate at Balliol, a classics teacher at Shrewsbury and a don at Trinity, Oxford). Indeed, he was an Oxford figure for half his life, and much invited to such societies. I would guess that it was he who made 'displacement activities' of this kind respectable . . . scholar yodelling to scholar across the groves of Academe as, in Wodehouse, aunt bellowed to aunt like mastodons across the primaeval swamp. Still . . . if you look at the last item in the book Wodehouse had published in 1903, *Tales of St Austin's*, you will find Wodehouse himself, as early as that, applying to *Tom Brown's Schooldays* mock-German-Homeric scholarship, and showing that the second, soppy, half of *Tom Brown* was written not by Hughes but by a group calling themselves The Secret Society for Putting Wholesome Literature within the Reach of Every Boy and Seeing That he Gets it.

Other notable contributions to Wodehouse scholarship? Well, I hope you've seen, in the cases outside dealing with the Empress of Blandings, the picture, found in a pig-breeding manual of the 1920s by a Wodehouse addict with the happy name of James Hogg . . . a picture of the Black Berkshire sow, painted by an artist named Wippell. It is very hard to argue for such a rare name, so appropriately connected, *not* having influenced Wodehouse. I personally believe, with James Hogg, that somehow Wodehouse had seen this book, this name and this picture of the black pig, and that the Empress was therefore specified as a Black Berkshire and Lord Emsworth's favourite author was given the crafty name Whiffle . . . his book being the immortal *On the Care of the Pig*. Go up top, James Hogg. And thank you, from all Wodehouse addicts.

By the way, another man, who shall be nameless because, alas, I have lost his letter, has discovered the author of *Types of Ethical Theory*. You will remember that this ghastly book was given to Bertie Wooster by the ghastly Florence Craye when they were first, and for the first time, engaged. And this is a passage that Bertie finds in it:

> The postulate or common understanding involved in speech is certainly coextensive, in the obligation it carries, with the social organism of which language is the instrument, and the ends of which it is an effort to subserve.

Bertie's comment, as narrator, is

> All perfectly true, no doubt; but not the sort of thing to spring on a lad with a morning head.

Bertie does not tell us the name of the author of this ghastly book. Frances Donaldson tells me that she showed the sentence quoted to Sir Isaiah Berlin, that polymath philosopher, at Oxford, and he couldn't identify the book or the author. But he did say that in philosophic jargon . . . the way philosophers talked and wrote when they were on the job . . . the sentence made some sense . . . it wasn't a parody. I am happy to report that the author is, or was, a Dr James Martineau, 1805–1900, referred to in the *Dictionary of National Biography* as a 'unitarian divine', and author of many philosophic books and treatises – none, alas, with any dialogue or pictures in them, I find – including one long essay on Spinoza, which I expect Jeeves has read. I tried it and got stuck in the second page. Dr Martineau achieved the distinction of having a book written about his work, entitled *Dr Martineau's Philosophy*, by one C. B. Upton. Just for fun I'd like to read you one thrilling passage in Upton's book:

> After distinguishing between a *spontaneity* and a *volition*, and explaining that for a voluntary act it is necessary that not less than two impulses should be present, Dr Martineau proceeds to express and establish a vital principle in his ethical theory, which is thus enunciated:
>
> > This plurality of simultaneous tendencies, however, would still present no cause for moral judgement were it not also felt to be a plurality of *simultaneous tendencies*. I must lay a separate stress upon each of those two words: a) the impulses must be simultaneous *inter se*: and b) they must be possibilities *to us*.

I could not bring myself to wade through *Types of Ethical Theory* to find the exact sentence that Bertie Wooster quoted. It is a very long book, and Dr Martineau is one of those philosophers who, for my money, disappear up their own hypotheses very quickly.

But I am delighted to learn, from Murphy again, that Plum Wodehouse's cousin, Helen Marion Wodehouse, Mistress of Girton College, Cambridge (where Florence Craye had been a student, of course) wrote books on philosophy too, and Murphy suggests, as a parallel to that passage from *Types of Ethical Theory* that Florence forced on to Bertie, this from Helen Marion Wodehouse's book, *The Logic of Will* . . .

> Of the two antithetic terms in the Greek philosophy only one was real and self-subsisting; and that one was Ideal Thought as opposed to that which it has to penetrate and mould. The other, corresponding to our Nature, was in itself phenomenal, unreal without any permanent footing, having no predicates that held true for two moments together; in short redeemed from negation only by including indwelling realities appearing through.

To compare . . . or perhaps correlate is the *mot juste* . . . Cousin Helen Marion Wodehouse with Lady Florence Craye is, with Murphy, the work of a moment, and I think he's got a real find there.

And now, as I come to the end of all this, there is one item of... well, call it scholarship – linguistic scholarship – in which the problem remains to be solved... and I give it to you in the wild hope that someone may spot the echo and give me the answer. May I ask you to listen very carefully... it's a slighter thing than that quotation from *Types of Ethical Theory*. It's a phrase, an idiom, an image . . . yes, an echo. I don't really know what a grammarian would call it. But Wodehouse uses it at least half a dozen times over the vintage years between the wars. He's echoing something. I *know* he's echoing something, parodying something, gently mocking something for his own amusement. I'll give you three examples . . . first Bertie, who is his own narrator as usual . . . he writes ' "Oh," I replied, with a suavity that became me well'. There's the little phrase that I am trying to locate . . . 'that became me well'. It's fatuous, and funny, and Wodehouse repeats it often enough in other contexts to make it significant. Here's another example, from a Mulliner story dealing with the Church . . . the story *Mulliner's Buck-U-Uppo*.

> His vicar glared at Augustine.
> 'What do you mean by jumping through my window?' he thundered. 'Are you a curate or a harlequin?'
> Augustine met his gaze with an unfaltering eye.
> 'I am a curate,' he replied with a dignity that well became him.

'With a suavity that became me well.' 'With a dignity that well became him.' I'll give you one more, from one of the golf stories:

> 'We want to settle a bet,' said James... 'will you please tell us who... I should say whom... you are knitting that sweater for?'
> 'It's not a sweater,' replied Miss Forester with a womanly candour that well became her. 'It's a sock.'

I think, and it's a guess, that this phrase, or turn of words, has a pulpit provenance... there's a churchy ring about it... the school chapel, the short manly sermon by an Old Boy Bishop? In my dreams I see young Wodehouse (P. G.) minor hearing it at Dulwich and making it part of a parody language for the student tea-party.

If you recognize and can identify this phrase, or turn of words, and tell me what it is echoing, I promise to see that your answer and your name is acknowledged, and distributed with gratitude to other Wodehouse scholars.

Well, I've overshot my time, and my subject, if any. But let me read to you . . . even if you read it yourself last Sunday in the *Sunday Times* Colour Magazine . . . what Arthur 'Call My Bluff' Marshall said at the end of that 'A Day In The Life Of' piece about him:

> I retire to bed very early, about half past nine. And every night before composing myself for sleep, I read a paragraph or two of P. G. Wodehouse. Because the writing is so perfect, the choice of words, the jokes, I always feel that I can go to sleep and, if I die in the night, there'll be this pleased expression on my face – a smile of quiet acceptance.

❧ ❧ ❧

Richard Usborne's Wodehouse At Work *was the first critical study of the books, and was published in 1961. When the author died thirteen years later, Usborne extended and revised his book as* Wodehouse At Work To The End. *He has adapted two Bertie/Jeeves novels as six-part plays for BBC radio, and has made an anthology,* Vintage Wodehouse. *Born in India in 1910, after Charterhouse and Oxford he worked in advertising and on magazines, spent most of the war years as an amateur soldier in the Middle East, and has recently retired after eight years with the National Trust as custodian of a lovely seventeenth-century house in Hampstead.*

WODEHOUSE IN THE THEATRE

by

William Douglas-Home

at the Lyttelton Theatre, 13 April 1982

LADIES and gentlemen, a week or so ago I had lunch with Sir Harold Hobson at the Ivy Restaurant. And the first thing he said to me, when I arrived, was 'When you deliver your lecture at the National Theatre on P. G. Wodehouse at 6 p.m. on the 13th of April' (these critics know everything!) 'are you going to read it or deliver it in the form of a speech?'

'Read it,' I said.

'Ah,' he said, 'Why?'

'Because', I said, 'it's meant to last between half an hour and forty-five minutes, which is too much to learn at my great age! And in any case, I've frequently watched the Dimbleby lectures on my Television, delivered by such distinguished figures as Sir Robert Mark, Lord Hailsham and Roy Jenkins, and they all read theirs, without exception.'

'Ah,' he said again.

'But why do you ask?' I said.

'Because', he said, 'I have to talk to the Eton College Literary Society at the end of the month, and the method of delivery I adopt will depend on the success or failure of the method you adopt on Tuesday.'

Well, it's nice to be of use to a dramatic critic who supported me for thirty years through thick and thin against the Philistines. So here goes!

THERE are two reasons why I am standing on a stage tonight in person, rather than in my normal role of being represented by actors – and both of them appear to me to be inadequate.

The first is because this course of talks on the subject of P. G. Wodehouse has been organized, on behalf of the National Theatre, by Giles Block, who came into my life, two or three years ago, when he was to have directed a play of mine in the

West End, starring Robert Morley. Morley withdrew from the production before it started, after treading on a jelly-fish in Australia, and has not been seen on the stage since – even though, as I understand it, the jelly-fish has been back at work for some time.

Well, it may be that Giles thought that he would compensate me for that disappointment by inviting me to make my début at the National tonight, albeit in an unaccustomed role.

And the second reason, no doubt, is because, about ten or fifteen years ago, I contributed an article, or an essay, or whatever you care to call it, to a volume entitled *Homage to P. G. Wodehouse*, published by Barrie and Jenkins and edited by Thelma Cazalet-Keir who was, as we all know, a close relative of Peter Cazalet, the race-horse trainer, who married Leonora, P. G. Wodehouse's stepdaughter, who died in 1944: to which sad event, her broken-hearted stepfather reacted by uttering the memorable phrase 'I thought she was immortal' and to whose memory this volume, with that tribute on the flyleaf, was affectionately dedicated.

Well, with those two dubious qualifications as my sponsors, I propose to divide this talk, as the historians tell us Caesar did with Gaul, into three parts – the first,which will be the shortest, being devoted to what is only the nodding aquaintanceship I had with the Wodehouse family – the second, which will be longer, being the most important, being devoted to the Wodehouse canon – and the third, which is only a facet of that all-embracing canon, only being given an airing because it is the subject of this talk.

Well, to start at the beginning with my limited contacts with the Wodehouse family, I used to meet Leonora before the war – and a very lovely girl she was. And I remember one occasion when I met her particularly vividly – not only because she was looking particularly lovely that evening at a ball at Fairlawne where her husband had his racing stable, but because, on my way to collect my car from the car park at three or four in the morning, I took the wrong turn, at the end of the garden, and stepped off a roof and fell twenty feet into the Stable Yard. And I remember being woken up early the next morning in the house where I was staying, by my brother Henry, who was also staying there, and being told to get up at once, because we were off to Le Touquet for the week-end in ten minutes. And I remember replying, 'Go away – for God's sake, I can't move, so I'm not coming.' And I remember my brother saying, 'Good God, don't tell me you fell off that roof into the Stable Yard too!' And I said 'What do you mean, too?' And he said, 'I said "too" because I did exactly the same thing on my way home just now!'

And I remember him limping out and shutting the door on his way to Le Touquet, where he met Leonora's mother and stepfather. This opportunity I missed, alas. My brother was made of sterner stuff than I was.

Well that was, so to speak, my only physical contact with the Wodehouse family and that is why I say that my reasons for standing here are inadequate, consisting as they do of a loose acquaintanceship with Giles Block (though not, I hasten to add, in the *Romans in Britain* sense), a near-fatal fall at Leonora Cazalet's pre-war party – and an essay in a volume published in honour of her stepfather's ninetieth birthday. And, added to those three inadequacies, I have to add a fourth, which is a confession that this is the first time, in a long life, that I have been called upon to give a talk – or a lecture (as it is described in my contract) – on any subject other than myself. And I'm bound to add, in all honesty, that I hope it will be the last, because it has caused me untold trouble.

After all, it is a comparatively simple matter for a writer – even a writer of dialogue, as opposed to prose – to compose a short essay on the subject of P. G. Wodehouse in the Theatre, which was the title of my contribution to the book I have already mentioned, as well as being the title of my talk tonight (according to the programme!). But it is a very different thing to enlarge an essay which takes only six or seven minutes to read, into a lecture lasting forty-five minutes, according to my contract, although, you will be pleased to hear, with dire penalties for exceeding that time limit (but with less dire penalties, I hope, for not reaching it!). And to have to do that standing on this awe-inspiring stage, which, whenever I have seen it before from the auditorium, has been peopled well with men and women, except possibly now I come to think of it, in the case of *Amadeus*, when it looked to be a fairly lonely spot, just as it is tonight – (as well as in the auditorium!).

In fact, I find myself strongly in sympathy with the sentiment expressed in a Wodehouse phrase, which was described as being one of his favourites by Lord David Cecil in his preface to the book I have already mentioned, when some character or other said, 'It is a very rummy feeling when you feel yourself braced for the fray and suddenly discover that the fray hasn't turned up!'

However, there is one grain of comfort in the whole situation which is that, having had to work on this talk for two or three weeks, it has been brought home to me that an essay is a very inadequate tribute to one of the greatest English writers of all time and that, far from being an unwelcome chore, it is, in fact, a great privilege to be allowed to comment at greater length on someone who was, beyond all doubt, a literary genius.

And the first comment I would make is to say how felicitous it was that Lord David Cecil should have ended his preface to that book of homage with a quotation from Evelyn Waugh – and how even more felicitous it was that the editor should have seen fit to close the book with an epilogue by Evelyn Waugh's son, Auberon.

And I make no apology for quoting from both of them (and I hasten to add that, in my present state of legal convalescence, I have permission from the surviving Waugh) because both express the unique contribution made by P. G. Wodehouse to English literature.

And not only, in my view, to literature, but also, which is marginally more important, to life – since he lived in an idyllic world and, with complete and also well-remunerated dedication, sold that idyll as a tonic to his readers.

Now, hear what Evelyn Waugh said, as quoted by David Cecil, in his preface to the book I have already mentioned.

> For Mr Wodehouse there has been no fall of Man: no 'aboriginal calamity'. His characters have never tasted the forbidden fruit. They are all still in Eden. The Gardens of Blandings Castle are that original garden from which we are all exiled. The chef Anatole prepares the ambrosia for the immortals of high Olympus. Mr Wodehouse's idyllic world can never stale.

Then, hear what Auberon wrote in his epilogue, and note that he goes even further than his father's tribute. He does not accept that we are exiled from the Blandings Castle gardens or indeed from Eden. He implies that we can dwell there still, if we are true disciples of the Wodehouse canon.

> 'Nobody', he writes, 'who has read through the Wodehouse canon can be left untouched by the radiant wisdom of its philosophy. And the practitioners of that philosophy,' (he goes on and I wouldn't argue with him) 'is that one society in England which is worth worrying about – the society of civilized and amiable people who have only a single qualification for membership – and that is an awareness of the Great English Joke.'
>
> 'And', he goes on, 'within the fellowship of the Great English Joke all seriousness – personal, religious, political – is reduced to absurdity.
>
> 'Alone among English writers, Mr Wodehouse has grasped the totality of the Great English Joke. The extent to which he has succeeded in implanting and fostering the idea of it in the British intelligentsia and professional classes, would alone make him the most influential novelist of our time, even if he did not happen to have done his implanting in four successive generations.
>
> 'My grandfather the critic, Arthur Waugh, would hold a handkerchief to his eyes as he read Wodehouse.
>
> 'My father used to read and reread the Wodehouse canon, year after year.
>
> 'My own youth and early manhood were entirely rescued by Wodehouse, saved from hideous error time and again.
>
> 'It is an enormous satisfaction to any parent when the children are seen safely in the bosom of a Wodehouse novel.'

Then he goes on to say – and all this is well-worth quoting since it hits the bull's-eye – that his claim that Wodehouse is the most influential novelist of our age does not of course mean that he has directly influenced political events, although occasionally the Conservative Party, in its more likeable moments, may give the impression of a Blandings Castle Preservation Society.

> 'The most profound effect he has had has been on the non-political intelligentsia, which effectively controls the margin within which our politicians can operate in the never-ending task they have set themselves, protecting their self-importance and compensating for whatever social and emotional deprivations makes this necessary.
>
> 'Mr Wodehouse's vineyard' – and this, in my view, is the most important single sentence ever written on the subject of that great man – 'Mr Wodehouse's vineyard is that little subversive corner in nearly every Englishman's heart, where he keeps his sense of the ridiculous.'

And it is important because it means that, once having read P. G. Wodehouse, one can never again be oppressed – as opposed to impressed, which one may still legitimately be – by the pomp and ceremony of life. As Auberon concludes – and this is my last quote from him – 'For those lucky people who have studied him, Wodehouse is present somewhere at every moment of the day.'

And I can personally vouch for the truth of that statement because my own father – and here I am going to start to quote from myself for a change – introduced me to the Wodehouse vineyard at a very early age.

And I make no apology for dwelling on the subject for a time, because it had a most profound effect on my career – and is therefore of great interest to me and, I like to think, to you!

My father used to go to Edinburgh every Tuesday in the years before the war, when I was a teenager or less – to a meeting of the British Linen Bank of which – in true conformity with the Wodehouse canon – he was Chairman.

And, at the conclusion of each meeting, he used to be given an envelope with ten pounds in it, on the outside of which he always wrote, in pencil, the word 'Money' and which, so far as I could see, was the only remuneration he ever received for sleeping through those meetings. Well, part of that money he used to spend on Edgar Wallace, who was rather more prolific than Wodehouse. But on red-letter days he used to return with the latest P. G. Wodehouse which he would slip to me when he got back home (probably having read it in the car) and which I used to devour immediately, in fair weather, under a rhododendron bush or, in wet weather, locked in the lavatory, to avoid the danger, which was always acute, of either of my elder brothers snatching it away.

And it is no exaggeration to say that from the first moment that my father brought the first P. G. Wodehouse back from Edinburgh, life changed for me, inevitably, as it later did for Auberon.

I'm not saying that it saved me, as it evidently did him, from 'hideous error time and again' – I still continued to indulge myself in such – but I am saying that it changed my whole outlook on society.

No longer was I overawed by butlers, bishops, statesmen, judges and the like – because I saw, beneath their bowler-hats, their mitres and their wigs, the vulnerable human beings that they were – like all the rest of us.

And I could laugh at them, instead of being overawed and, what's more, laugh at them, not cruelly, but in sympathy and understanding.

And the second most important thing that I discovered – and much to my delight – was that my own home was like a Wodehouse novel – with my father standing in for Lord Emsworth and his butler, Mr Collingwood, standing in for Jeeves and 'Hairy Mary', as we used to call her, who was, in reality, my father's sister Mary – standing in for Lady Constance, in that she could talk the hind leg off a donkey, too!

As a consequence of this discovery, I found myself in Eden and, to tell the truth, I've stayed there ever since, with no regrets.

In my considered view, the alchemy dispensed by P. G. Wodehouse works as follows. It does NOT, as superficial students of such things imagine, blind you to reality and leave you living in a kind of punch-drunk and euphoric stupor, unaware of what is going on around you on this unattractive planet.

On the contrary, it sharpens your perception and enables you to discern, with increased awareness, all the follies which mankind is heir to.

But it also gives you the ability to tolerate them, by applying, as the younger Waugh suggests, the Wodehouse canon to them.

For example, in the war – and here I open my soul to you – I discovered that it was most helpful to the preservation of my sanity to think, at least three times a week, of Hitler – not between Field-Marshal Goering and Field-Marshal Keitel, on a rostrum with the whole might of the German Army marching past him, in his uniform and with his right arm lifted in salute, but sitting in his bath – the soap in one hand and his flannel in the other, with the nail-brush in the soap-tray and its understudy on his upper lip.

Now this protective mechanism which, throughout those long years, kept me more or less sane – some might argue less rather than more – was a direct result of reading P. G. Wodehouse in my early youth.

And not only in the field of foreign politics did I apply this lesson. I applied it, when the war was over, to domestic politics as well and thus embarked on the profession by which I have made my living ever since.

And all this, I repeat, because I learned the Wodehouse canon in my early youth – which canon, I also repeat, requires one to investigate beneath the surface till one finds a peg on which to hang one's sense of the ridiculous.

And thus I learned to look beneath the surface of my father's Lord Lieutenantship and find the man beneath the ermine. And I also learned to look beneath his butler, Mr Collingwood's tail-coat, and spot the Tory politician lurking there.

From that it was a simple step to write *The Chiltern Hundreds* – thanks, I now most gratefully acknowledge, at this late date – to the Wodehouse canon.

But I must not leave my father's contribution out, because it was enormous. My study of him was inspired by Wodehouse; but in some respects he excelled Lord Emsworth, in that he was working on a larger canvas. A lot of my plays, starring 'elderly' eccentric gentlemen, like Lord-Lieutenants, retired Generals and members of the Jockey Club, owe almost everything to him. In fact, I think it likely that I've made more voyages around my father than John Mortimer has ever wotted of.

To give you one example of my father's eccentricity – if I may divert momentarily from my theme – I'll tell you of a visit he made to me, with my mother, when I was in Wakefield Gaol in 1944.

My mother, as she told me later, got into the taxi which was to return them to York Station, while my father started walking down outside the prison wall, towards a big house.

'Here's our taxi, Charlie,' called my mother. 'Hold on a minute, Lil,' my father said, as he strode on, 'I'm just going to thank the dear little Governor for having Willie here.'

I question whether Lord Emsworth could have topped that as an exercise in gentle eccentricity.

And that is why I put my father in a dead-heat with the Wodehouse canon, as contributor in chief to any inspiration – *pace* the dramatic critics! – that I may have had – or may have yet – in my theatrical career.

Another thing that Wodehouse taught me – which perhaps is even more important than the exercising of one's sense of the ridiculous: a lesson which I often wish more than a handful of dramatic critics could absorb – is that the perfect, and, indeed, the only, background for such exercises in the art of gentle unmalicious ridicule, is the environment which P. G. Wodehouse chose – the playground of what sociologists would call the leisured classes: those who have inherited a bit of money: those who've made their pile at one time or another: those who have augmented that pile by astute investment or an equally enlightened marriage: those who have all but got through it: those who dwell in stately homes whether supported by the National Trust or not: those who lunch in clubs in Pall Mall or St James's Street: those who, like Bertie Wooster, still have valets: those who, like a Duke or two that I have stayed with, still have butlers.

Now that handful of dramatic critics that I mentioned earlier – no names, no pack-drill, except, of course, that pack-drill which has always been my lot and which, without undue discomfort, has now worn into my shoulder – this handful of dramatic critics (as opposed to literary critics who are much more sensible) entirely fail to understand that authors, whether they be novelists or playwrights, quite deliberately write about such people, not because such writers are old-fashioned, or effete or snobbish, but because they know, instinctively, that only in such soil can the twin seeds of gentle ridicule and tender satire flourish to perfection, and thus yield a bumper harvest, if allowed to do so.

And the reason why such writers choose this background is because only the leisured classes have the opportunity to be eccentric since they have the time and, some of them, the space in which to exercise it and the income to support it. Nor are they, as some suppose, a dying breed. Indeed the field has widened. In the past it was the aristocracy, but now, according to the politicians, we are starting on the age of leisure in the last years of this century. It follows, therefore, that, so far from being the last remnants of a dying breed, the leisured classes, the eccentric and – to put it in a nutshell – the nut-cases will increase and multiply, providing future Wodehouses with even richer soil than he worked and with even richer harvests.

And not only novelists like Wodehouse, be it said, but dramatists as well – always provided they are not accused of flogging a dead horse or trying to resuscitate a dodo, when, in fact, they are prospecting, with complete propriety and proper dedication and professional integrity, what is without a doubt the richest seam of comedy available to any writer, in the theatre or out of it.

And this, of course, brings me to what is advertised as my main theme – the influence of P. G. Wodehouse on the theatre. But first I'd like to add one tribute to him as a novelist – which I may be allowed to lay beside the wreaths of David Cecil and the two Waughs on his cenotaph.

This tribute is not from me, since I've paid mine already, but from Monty James, the Provost of Eton in the days when I was there. He was a distinguished literary figure and a scholar of such awe-inspiring erudition, that I still tremble at the thought of meeting him, which, in fact, I never did, because I was too young and insignificant.

Or, to be more accurate, I used to tremble up to ten or fifteen years ago, when I met a successor of Dr James, as a result of which my awe of Provosts of Eton was finally exorcised. And I make no apology for telling you of it, since it comes well within the Wodehouse canon, in that it illustrates the delight of looking underneath the trappings and discovering the true man.

I went to stay with Celia and Peter Fleming for the night at their home at Merrimoles shortly before Peter died. When I arrived Celia said 'Peter and Harold Caccia are up in the billiard-room. So take a drink up with you.'

I did as she bid me and, half-way up the stairs, I thought to myself, 'My God, I'm going to meet a Provost of Eton, and if he's anything like as imposing and awe-inspiring as was Dr James – I'm going to be a jelly. So I'd better reinforce myself.' So I took a huge swig of whisky and, emboldened somewhat, I went on up the stairs, opened the door of the billiard-room gently and, as I did so, a voice rang out. It wasn't Peter Fleming's and what it said, loud and clear, was, 'Get into that pocket, you little red sod!'

From that date I have no longer been in awe of Provosts of Eton, because I have found out that, true to the Wodehouse canon, they are human beings underneath, like all the rest of us.

Well, to return to my theme, it was Dr James who once remarked, with all the weight of his scholarship behind him, that P. G. Wodehouse's command of the English language was unrivalled. And when Dr James used the word unrivalled, he meant nothing less than unrivalled which, freely translated, means unique.

And he went on to say that no matter that Wodehouse's themes were flippant and his characters inane, his English was impeccable and his descriptive powers inimitable. And when Dr James used the word 'inimitable' it meant exactly that, which also by definition means unique.

We may therefore, I think, supported by all these big guns, accept the fact that as a writer of English prose he was in a class of his own.

The question therefore arises – and here I come not only to the subject of my talk but very nearly to the conclusion of it – the question then arises whether P. G. Wodehouse was also in a class of his own in the theatre.

Before I wrote my contribution to *Homage to P. G. Wodehouse*, I have to confess that I had no idea that he had made any contribution to the theatre at all. When I sat down to write that article I had heard myself saying to myself 'Honestly, old egg' (which was the phrase he always used when corresponding with his stepdaughter) 'Honestly, old egg, I don't know where to begin.' Indeed, if it hadn't been for Edward Cazalet (Leonora's son) and Christopher MacLehose (of Barrie and Jenkins), Wodehouse's friend Gerard Fairlie and, last but not least, John Chapman (who adapted a book of Wodehouse's for the stage), I never would have begun at all.

But, with infinite kindness, they supplied me with dates and data and letters which informed me, to my astonishment, that between 1915 and 1928 he had been involved – primarily as a lyric-writer, though often, also, on the book – in the production of no fewer than eighteen musical comedies, most of which were highly successful on both sides of the Atlantic.

But I have to confess that the piece of information that intrigued me most was that, on one occasion, he achieved what has always been one of my Walter Mittys – he actually reviewed one of his own productions, which was called *Miss Springtime*. His review of it, in *Vanity Fair*, started:

> I feel a slight diffidence about growing enthusiastic over *Miss Springtime* for the fact is that, having contributed a few lyrical bijous to the above (just a few trifles, you know, dashed off in the intervals of more serious work) I am drawing a royalty from it which already has caused the wolf to move up a few parasangs from the Wodehouse doorstep.

So much for the musicals – but what about the plays?

In the mid-twenties his musical output, though far from over, was slowing down and he was flirting with the straight theatre – indeed, more than flirting, since his efforts, as always, were attended by success.

He made an adaptation of a German play: then an adaptation of a French play (which made Leslie Howard a star): and then, so far as I can ascertain, he wrote a play called *Good Morning, Bill* on his own.

> 'How refreshing it is,' a dramatic critic wrote, 'to laugh in a theatre with one whose humour is neither blatant nor coarse nor cruel: whose silliness, when he is silly, has the gold sting of character to save it, and whose sense of nonsense has an easy graceful good humour which makes unnecessary the noisy violence which is too often the only support of fame.'

And he concluded, in unconscious support of Dr James's accolade, 'The matter is this – Mr Wodehouse has style!'

But *Good Morning, Bill* seems to be almost the only play he did write on his own. He dramatized *A Damsel in Distress* with Ian Hay, in which, according to him, 'Ian hogged it all'. He collaborated with Ian Hay on *Baa, Baa, Black Sheep* (from a story 'the Hogger' wrote himself). This production made Gertrude Lawrence a star. And then in 1930 he again collaborated with Ian Hay on a dramatization of *Leave it to Psmith*.

Then there was a gap of forty years before the next theatrical collaboration. The reason for this prolonged hiatus, in my judgement, is that – apart from the exception which proves the rule in the shape of *Good Morning, Bill* – he was not, when it came to the crunch, a playwright, but a novelist. And, what is more – and this, I submit, is the heart of the matter – he could not convert himself into a playwright because he was, quite simply, too good a writer of prose.

And the question, I suggest, that one should ask oneself is 'Can a writer of that calibre become a writer in the theatre?

Is not switching such a prose artist into the writing of dialogue rather like expecting Lester Piggott to do well in motorcycle races? Would not such a change of life destroy his genius, removing from him his magic touch with horses?'

So with Wodehouse's descriptive powers.

In that article I wrote for *Homage to P. G. Wodehouse* I quoted a passage from what, at that time, I imagined to be one of his books, although since then I'm bound to confess that Lady Donaldson has told me that she can't trace it anywhere. It must have been a figment of my imagination. Never mind, it illustrates the point that I am making. (And indeed since, according to my contract, I am not allowed to quote, it may be just as well that I invented it!)

Well, in this extract, fictitious or otherwise, a young girl came out on to the verandah. Her father stood at his easel, in the orchard.

'Hullo, Daddy,' she said. 'What are you doing?'

'Painting, my dear,' he replied, for there were no secrets between these two.

Well now try to dramatize that and you will see the point that I am trying to make.

'Hullo, Daddy, what are you doing?'

'Painting, my dear. I'm telling you because there are no secrets between us.'

The fact is that it can't be done. Perfection cannot be adapted to another medium.

To give another example – and here I am going to stick my neck out and give a direct quote, though paraphrased, from P. G. Wodehouse (and thus risk a prosecution, not from Mrs Whitehouse but Sir Peter Hall!) when he wrote about a young man whose proposal to his girl-friend on a summer evening behind a hedge was drowned by the thunderous roar of butterflies landing and taking off on the adjoining meadow. Well, how can such a pearl as that be translated into dialogue – no matter who the actor who is asked to speak it?

Wodehouse had another go in the theatre forty years after collaborating with Ian Hay in *Leave it to Psmith.* It was when John Chapman adapted *Blandings Castle* to the stage and the play was produced by Peter Saunders under the name of *Oh, Clarence!*

I would like to conclude with some extracts from some of the letters Wodehouse wrote to John Chapman. The latter kindly supplied me with them for my original article. And I quote from them to illustrate the kind of man Wodehouse was, aged, let it be remembered, eighty-eight.

'Aug. 3
Dear John,

Your cable came as Manna in the W. I think *Blandings Castle* which I have now read six times is the most brilliant play ever written, but I had been feeling a bit uneasy because, in this proletarian age, I was afraid a play about the aristocracy might be resented. If Manchester likes it, everybody will like it.

All the best,
Yours ever,
Plum.'

'Aug. 23rd
Dear John,

This is instead of a firstnight telegram. One can say so little in a t. It was wonderful having the talk on the transatlantic phone – let's have some more!

I haven't heard the return from Brighton yet, but I'm sure they know what's good for them down there, and haven't let us down. What an amazing road tour. There surely can't have been another like it. If we get over the 28th with a bang, I feel sure we can get a Broadway production. So here's hoping.

All the best,
Yours ever,
Plum.

PS. At the end of Act II? Do you have a real pig?'

'Oct. 9th
Dear John,

What a stinker that was in *Punch*. I hope it did not depress you. It hasn't made the slightest difference to the business apparently, and it certainly hasn't made me change my view that you have written the best play that could possibly be done on B. Castle. Today your agent sent me the figures to date and one couldn't want anything more solid.'

'Feb. 19
Dear John,

I got the bad news before your letter arrived. My sister-in-law's sister rang up the box office to buy seats for the 10th Feb., and was told that the show was closing on the 8th. It's sad, but after all we had a run of about 160 performances and nobody could be ashamed of that. . . . As you say, it ought to be good repertory and amateurs. Anyway, I cling to my opinion that you did a terrific job and I shall go on reading the script indefinitely.

Meanwhile, I hope *Not Now, Darling* [by John Chapman and Ray Cooney] is going as strong as ever. Though I have a feeling that its triumphant success followed by two more of your shows influenced the critics against you, they being the lice they are.'

Well, are they lice? And this is me talking now – not Wodehouse. I've thought so in my time myself and I confess I've said so too, which didn't do me any good at all. But are they? On mature reflection, I don't think so. Sometimes some of them are prejudiced politically or socially or both: but most of them, in my experience, attempt to do a hard job well and quite a few of them succeed.

What was it put them off *Oh, Clarence!*, then? Could it have been the fact I touched on when I started – namely that however hard John Chapman tried to dramatize the Wodehouse characters – and he succeeded brilliantly – he could not dramatize the Wodehouse genius which lies (forgive the repetition, since this is important) in his quite inimitable style – in his descriptive powers – in short, in his prose.

That, I think, is what the critics, in their wisdom, found in short supply – through no one's fault, of course, because prose necessarily has no place in dialogue.

But nonetheless it was a noble effort and the writer of those letters clearly spotted that and said so, although I suspect that he knew just as well as I do (and I'm sure an expert like John Chapman knows it too), that any dramatist who tries to dramatize the works of a prose writer with the genius of Wodehouse carries too much weight for comfort – or, to put it with more accuracy, loses too much.

So much for the plays, then. What about the letter writer? Was there ever such a lively fellow in his age group? I take leave to doubt it. Was there ever such enthusiasm, such unselfishness, such charity as shines through all those letters?

Honestly – and this is my last word – it's hard to think of any old egg I admire more.

❧ ❧ ❧

Hon. William Douglas-Home. Born 1912. Eton, Oxford and Royal Academy of Dramatic Art. He has been an actor on West End stages. As a dramatist, he has written more than thirty plays that have been performed and published. He has stood unsuccessfully for Parliament three times. He has written two books of autobiography. In the Army, he was court-martialled and cashiered in 1944, with one year's imprisonment with hard labour, for refusing to attack Le Havre after the German Commander's request to be allowed to evacuate civilians before the battle had been refused.

IN TIME OF TROUBLE

by
Malcolm Muggeridge

at the Lyttelton Theatre, 28 April 1982

THIS is, in a way, rather a fraudulent appearance on my part; I am by no means an expert on Wodehouse's writings, nor even a fanatical admirer of them. I have derived much enjoyment from them, but I don't have the addiction that an Orwell or Evelyn Waugh had. It is, however, true that I came to be involved in what may well have been the only truly tragic moment in Wodehouse's life, and I shall content myself with describing how he reacted to these unusual circumstances, what was their outcome, and how we got along together.

We met in Paris at the time of its *soi-disant* liberation in August 1944; Wodehouse was staying at the Bristol Hotel and I was a liaison officer with the French *Sécurité Militaire*. He was in sore trouble because of the broadcasts he had given from Berlin, and I had been instructed to make contact with him. Before, however, going into all that, I should perhaps say something about the circumstances in France, particularly in Paris, when chance brought us together.

Wodehouse was living quietly in the Bristol Hotel, but France as a whole, and Paris in particular, was in a considerable state of chaos. Fighting continued in the streets, and the war, which was over as the war against Germany, was only beginning in regard to the struggle within France as to who would emerge to take charge. De Gaulle arrived in France and made his way to Paris. Rather to the consternation of his Anglo-American allies, everywhere he went he was accepted as the personification of authority. All the plans that had been made by the Allies to hold elections before setting up a French government – having, in other words, a Military Government for a period of time – fell to the ground because this extraordinary man just arrived on the scene, and automatically, became the government. At the same time, in Paris particularly, but also all over France, there was a sort of civil war going on.

On the one hand there were the forces called FFI (*Forces Françaises Intérieures*), which were really a revolutionary force of the extreme Left ready to take over, and, on the other, you had all the people who had been living in Occupied France, and who, in that they had been living there and had carried on their normal lives, were open to the charge of collaborating with the enemy. There was an enormous lot of working off of particular hatreds between people or between groups of people in the name of this so-called *Épuration*, or Purification. It was a time of chaos, a time when there was no law because the law that existed, the courts that existed, the judges that existed, were tainted with Pétainism, and therefore discredited in the circumstances of the ending of the war. Similarly, the police were tarred with the same brush, and therefore, since there was no law or law enforcement, there were infinite possibilities for working off private hatreds, for political scheming and for sheer gangsterism.

I came over to France with two officers of the *Sécurité Militaire* in the very early part of the Liberation. We were unable to land at Le Bourget because there was still fighting there, so we landed in a field – we had a small 'plane from Heathrow, myself and these two officers – and then managed to get on to a truck which drove us into Paris. As we went along we were received with enthusiasm and handed refreshing drinks, greeted with flowers and with smiles, as though we were liberators; by the time we reached Paris I think we really thought that we were. When we got to Paris I was able to make contact with other British Intelligence officers who were there, and we dossed down in the Petit Palais. I remember very well wandering round with some friends on the first evening, and, finding that the night-clubs on the Left Bank were still going, we ventured into one of them. A clown with an enormous solemn face – I can see him now – was doing a turn which ended with his saying in a voice of infinite melancholy: '*Et maintenant nous sommes libérés*'. I felt it was the right note.

The following morning Trevor Wilson, an MI6 officer who had also arrived from London, said that he had been given a list of various people who were to be seen and accounted for; they were people who were reputed to be fifth columnists or spies or double agents, and he suggested that, as a person who, in civilian life, earned my living by writing, I might care to deal with the case of P. G. Wodehouse. I eagerly seized on this opportunity, partly because a sort of Trades Unionism gave me the feeling that someone who had written as many successful books as Wodehouse had, really shouldn't be interfered with unduly, and partly because I felt an enormous curiosity to see him and to hear what he had to say.

I am sure you all know what had happened, but in case any of you don't I'll explain briefly. When he was released from the internment camp at Tost in Poland – formerly a lunatic asylum, as he was delighted to learn – it was intimated to him that it might be a good idea if he were to talk to his American readers on the short wave radio. America was not, at that time, at war with Germany, and Wodehouse, who was always very interested in his readers, especially his American readers, thought that this would be a wonderful thing; they hadn't heard of him for some years, and this would be a very nice way of reminding them that he was still around and still writing books. So he agreed to do this, and prepared five broadcasts. I had occasion to read them later, and was able to satisfy myself that there was absolutely nothing in them that could possibly be described as treason. They were simply a rather typical Wodehousian, amusing account of everything that had happened to him from the moment the Germans arrived at Le Touquet where he was living. He was then less than sixty, and therefore of military age and subject to internment, and he gave accounts of the stages of his journey to Poland, and his time in the camp. He described the guards, his fellow-prisoners and the way in which, in his inimitable manner, every morning out came an old typewriter, and there he was tapping away, to the great interest of the German guards. Blissfully unconscious of what was happening in the world, or at any rate not unduly worrying about it, he could tap out his daily quota of words, and this he proceeded to do.

Of course, the broadcasts created a terrific uproar in England. Those of you who are young won't remember it, but it did sound awfully bad. The Germans were occupying the whole of France. London had been blitzed and it had looked as though England was to be invaded at any moment. Germany had invaded Russia. All this, and suddenly on the air there comes this amusing, aloof, as I said, characteristic Wodehousian account of what had been happening to him. There was a tremendous reaction, particularly on the part of his fellow-writers. They were utterly enraged. I think that perhaps they had been a little envious of Wodehouse's success, and resented the fact that, though he was regarded as a humorous writer, he had been given a doctorate at Oxford University. Anyway, there he was – Dr Wodehouse; always punctiliously so addressed by Evelyn Waugh. Then suddenly he appears to be on the enemy's side. Let us admit that it was an act of near insanity on his part not to have foreseen how the German radio was bound to ensure the transmission of his broadcasts on other channels, thereby giving the impression that he was *persona grata* in Berlin.

The then Minister of Information, Duff Cooper, decided that Wodehouse should be publicly attacked and repudiated. At the time there was a columnist on the *Daily Mirror* who signed himself Cassandra. Actually, he was a man called Bill Connor, an Irishman who has long ago been gathered to his fathers, but in those days was a pretty vituperous person. He went on BBC radio and really gave Wodehouse the works. In the Letters columns of the *Daily Telegraph* other writers, such as A. A. Milne, E. C. Bentley and Sean O'Casey, wrote extraordinarily abusive letters, particularly those people who had adulated Wodehouse the most. It's a strange thing that there is nothing that so enrages human beings as to feel that they have been unprofitably adulatory. The same thing happened, I remember very well, when King Edward VIII gave up the throne; all the people who had been adulating him turned and rent him with particular fury because they felt they had been cheated into adulating him. There is no surer way of becoming the target of one's fellow humans' rage than to have been adulated by them.

That was how matters stood when I went to see Wodehouse at the Paris Bristol Hotel. There was a very respectable-looking receptionist there in a cut-away coat, and I told him I had come to see Monsieur Wodehouse. He didn't display the slightest anxiety or excitement at a British officer arriving and saying that he wished to see Monsieur Wodehouse. You know, there's a funny thing about wars that is often overlooked;

one's always talking about the enormous destructiveness of wars, but also it's amazing the number of things that still carry on notwithstanding. There was this man, in his black swallow-tail coat, extremely respectfully intimating that I could go up and see Monsieur Wodehouse. Thinking it over afterwards I realized that he was not such a fool as to suppose that, just because at this moment Monsieur Wodehouse might be in bad trouble, he would not later on be a desirable client. The Bristol Hotel would go on needing rich and famous people to come and stay there. Wodehouse was indubitably a rich and famous person, and therefore it was as well to keep on good terms with him.

As it happened, I came to be billeted in the Rothschild mansion in the Avenue Marigny. Victor Rothschild, a fellow-Intelligence officer, had prudently requisitioned his ancestors' mansion, and then he had to fill it up with British officers to make sure that there was no other intrusion. What I found quite extraordinary was that the house had been occupied by a German Luftwaffe general, and I was amazed to see that its furniture and pictures, which were doubtless very valuable, were all nonetheless intact. The general in question, Von Alvensleben, had left everything in perfect order. There was a rather sharp little man, Monsieur Félix, who looked after the door – a very heavy door. I mentioned to him that I had been surprised that a house owned by one of the most famous Jewish families in the world should be occupied by a German general and not be in any way touched or harmed. Monsieur Félix looked at me quizzically and delivered himself of this saying: 'Hitlers come and go, but Rothschilds go on for ever'. There is a lot of that particular sentiment in war; I sensed it in Paris, and felt it very strongly in the Bristol Hotel.

The lift wasn't working, and I climbed up to Wodehouse's floor. Obviously the receptionist had telephoned him, and he was expecting me. In I went, and he was standing there, a very large man dressed in grey flannel trousers and sports coat, looking rather like a prep-school master of the old school. He was smiling, not a bit embarrassed. We sat down. I was supposed to be questioning him, but he started by asking me all sorts of questions. What was on in the London theatres? Did *The Times Literary Supplement* still come out? I said, alas, yes, and so on, until, finally, I had to broach the question of the broadcasts. I told him that, of course, I had come on that account, that I didn't know how far he was *au fait* with what had been going on, but that there had been very strong feelings, and that I, as a British Intelligence officer, had been sent along to see him and raise certain questions. I thought it might be a good idea to raise the matter of the legal position; I did this because it usually makes people go numb when they hear that there is a legal position that has to be looked into. Needless to say, I knew nothing about it myself. We sat there talking, and it's a strange thing, but my most vivid memory of the scene, as I speak to you about it now, is the almost mystical sense I had of the peace in that room where I was sitting with the alleged traitor whom I was supposed to deal with, while outside there was the shooting and the shouting, and all the manifestations of violence and disorder. As night came on, and we went on talking away, I grew more than ever aware of the peace inside the room by contrast with what was going on outside. And I think it was this that, more than anything else, made me feel from the beginning, not exactly on Wodehouse's side, but that he had aligned himself against all the shooting and the shouting that was going on outside, and I could not but admire how he diligently, methodically, regularly, continued to ply his trade as a writer.

Now, fortunately for me, MI5 sent out a lawyer named Cussen. He was dressed up in uniform, but he was unmistakably a lawyer, and had the peculiar way that lawyers have of speaking down his nose; what is being said sort of comes out from the nose rather than the mouth. He very honestly and correctly went into the whole matter, and he too decided that there was no charge that could be made against Wodehouse, that what he had done was foolish and improper, but that there was nothing that would be the occasion for a serious charge. His report was duly filed, and, for some mysterious reason which I still don't understand, it was withheld from the public even when the thirty-year limit was passed. There was some extraordinary story of there being some name in the report which shouldn't be known, but anyway I read it when he prepared it, and could not see any reason why it should be withheld.

That's how things were, and how Wodehouse and I got to know each other. We used to go for walks together. Then one morning I received a telephone call from Jacqueline de Broglie. She was half French, half American. Her mother was a rather famous social figure called Daisy Fellowes who belonged to the Singer Sewing Machine family, and so was enormously rich. Jacqueline telephoned to tell me that, the night before, the Wodehouses had been arrested, and were in custody at the police station in the Quai d'Orléans. I said I would go along there. In the particular circumstances of Paris at that time, to be a British officer connected with the *Sécurité Militaire* gave one a certain standing which one certainly wouldn't otherwise have had, and so I went into the police station and said that I had come about Monsieur Wodehouse, and could I please see him? Ethel Wodehouse was there with their Pekinese dog, Wonder, and I had a very strong feeling that the police wanted that dog out of the place. So it wasn't very difficult to persuade them that Mrs Wodehouse and the dog should be allowed to go, and off they went, leaving Wodehouse there.

The police hadn't the faintest idea who Wodehouse was – they even spelt his name wrongly – or why he was there. What had happened had been that the then *Préfet*, a man called Luiset, had given a dinner party, and an English lady who was present – I never knew her name – said, in the course of the evening, that it was an absolute scandal that P. G. Wodehouse should be walking about free in Paris. Whereupon Luiset immediately sent instructions that Wodehouse should be arrested and three of his men in black shining jackets turned up in the middle of the night and took the Wodehouses along to the Quai d'Orléans.

Wodehouse himself remained in custody, and it was intimated to me, in that extraordinarily frank way that the French have, that the only way they could ameliorate his circumstances would be if he was ill, for then he could be put in a clinic. A doctor was called, who took his temperature; it was normal, but we all agreed that Wodehouse was in a poor way. The only place where there was an available bed turned out to be in a maternity ward! The extraordinary thing about this story is that it is a sort of Wodehousian story; it's as though he had written it himself. His first place of internment – Tost – was a lunatic asylum; now every morning he sat up in a maternity ward with his typewriter, writing his books. There were two gendarmes to ensure that he did not escape; in the evenings they played cards together. Such was his life there, and one had the feeling that he would have been perfectly happy to stay on in the maternity ward indefinitely.

However, I went to see Duff Cooper who, as Minister of Information, had mounted the attack on Wodehouse in the first place. Now he was the British Ambassador in Paris. I indicated that, in my opinion, it would be disastrous if Wodehouse were sent back to London. You see, what I had gathered from the police was that they would propose sending him back to London. In the particular temper of that time, this could have been a very serious matter. Don't forget that Joyce, the broadcaster called Lord Haw-Haw, was executed for his pro-German propaganda even though he was, in fact, not a British subject – he was an American subject. He had a British passport, which he had procured by fraudulent means, and he was executed for not being loyal to a passport he had no right to – a strange business. Likewise, things could have been very serious for Wodehouse if he had been sent back to London, and, in so far as I played any crucial part in this story of Wodehouse, it was in trying to prevent that happening. I spoke to Duff Cooper about it, and he was inclined to agree. I pointed out to him that, all unknown to himself, Wodehouse had in fact made one very great contribution to the war effort. The Germans (it's hard to believe this, I know) had the idea that from Wodehouse's writings they could learn and simulate the behaviour of an English gentleman. This sounds very far-fetched, but it's true. An unfortunate German was landed by parachute in the Fen country to be an agent, whereupon he was immediately arrested – not surprisingly, for he was wearing spats! I felt sorry in a way that he was arrested so soon. Otherwise, presumably, he would have gone to London and asked where was the Drones Club, and perhaps hoped to escape notice in its dining-room by throwing bread about. Anyway, Wodehouse was not sent to London. Duff Cooper agreed that both what I said and what Cussen said indicated that it would be quite ridiculous to send him to London at this time, since there was no serious charge against him, simply a charge of carelessness and, in a sense, idiocy. I drove Wodehouse out to Fontainebleau, where he and Ethel and the dog, Wonder, were settled in a hotel. There I said goodbye to them.

It was only after the war, when I was a newspaper correspondent in Washington, that I saw him again. By that time he was established in Remsenberg, in Long Island. He was hard at work turning out his books, which were still being very successful, and we talked about our encounter at the Bristol Hotel, and his subsequent adventures. I tried to make out what he had really felt through this experience, how it had hurt him, what he had felt inside himself, and what in retrospect it really signified. Very characteristically, he said that what he'd felt like was as though he'd been a wonderfully popular comedian, and then he goes on the stage, he opens his mouth, and he gets the bird. That was how he saw the whole episode. I think, however, that he *was* hurt, too; there were, inevitably, scars left by it. To be the target of collective rage (I have experienced this myself, although not nearly to the degree that he did) . . . there is something particularly terrible about being the target of collective rage. That mysterious chap, Kierkegaard, says that ten thousand people all shouting out the same thing makes it false even if it happens to be true. I understand what he means by that. Wodehouse was for a time the target of collective fury; later, of course, he became once more the target of collective sycophancy, and the lavish celebration of his eightieth birthday, and the knighthood that he received six weeks before he died, perhaps solaced him. Perhaps, though, he worked out in his mind how these two – first, the collective fury, and then the collective adulation – cancel out, and wondered whether there was all that difference between them.

On Long Island there was the same routine. He described it in a television interview I did with him about this time as follows: 'I wake up at about eight, and then I do three-quarters of an hour's exercise, shave and have a bath and everything, have breakfast and then I start work which I have to knock off at twelve because I want to see a television show called *Edge of Night* which ruins my morning's work. Then lunch. Then I take the dogs for a walk. We've got a dachshund and a boxer, and I have to take them for a walk; then I work again until five. Later I have a cocktail, dinner – very early dinner for the sake of the help – and I generally read most of the rest of the evening.' After a thoughtful pause he added: 'It sounds awfully dull, yet it isn't'. He went on to the very end in the same way, and in almost the last letter he wrote, when he was virtually on his deathbed, he said: 'My Jeeves novel has been in the best-seller list ever since it came out. I am well on in a new Blandings Castle novel which looks good so far.' So he arrived at the Celestial Gate having carried on his way of life to the very end, and I must say that if I were to look for his epitaph, the one that comes to my mind is Dr Johnson's on Garrick: 'I am disappointed by that stroke of death which has eclipsed the gaiety of nations and impoverished the public stock of harmless pleasure'. I think that would be a nice thing to say of Wodehouse. Certainly, he did produce much public pleasure, and I feel very happy that in the one horrible, ugly episode I was able to render a little help, if only in the negative sense of preventing his going to London, where he might have been – in the rage then prevailing – torn to pieces.

❦ ❦ ❦

Malcolm Muggeridge, born 1903, went, after Cambridge, as Lecturer at the Egyptian University in Cairo. He has been a journalist in Russia, India, Washington and London, and his attachment, during the war, to MI6 took him to South and North Africa and to Paris after the Liberation in 1944. He was Editor of Punch *for four years in the 1950s. He was Rector of Edinburgh University for a year in the 1960s. He is well known as a broadcaster, on radio and television. He has written novels, plays, biographies, diaries and autobiographies. He was received into the Roman Catholic Church in 1982. He lives in Sussex and in past years used to frequent the South of France in winter.*

AFTER-DINNER WODEHOUSE
by
Angus Macintyre

at Strand House, 6 April 1982

Your Majesty, Ladies and Gentlemen:

In my experience, dons are good at pretending to know more than they do – as good at this as bankers and lawyers, better at it than politicians; but before the company assembled to-night, I will not even attempt such pretence. For the company includes Frankie Donaldson, Wodehouse's biographer, the perfect choice for the job, both because of her stature as a writer and her deep, instinctive understanding of her subject; and Richard Usborne, the man who has done more to elucidate the work of Wodehouse than anyone else alive – and who has done so with grace, accuracy and proper feeling. I see around me many others whose correspondence course on Wodehousian matters I could take with profit. I feel as much of a fraud and almost as daunted as Bertie Wooster was on the occasion when Miss Tomlinson, the headmistress of the girls' school, asked Bertie – at the Machiavellian prompting of Jeeves – to say a few words to her girls: she told him to 'be bright and amusing' but not to 'neglect the graver note'. What was needed was something 'brave and helpful and stimulating' – good, crisp advice for any public speaker. All Bertie can manage, after a visibly painful effort to make his brain work, is to offer the girls his Uncle Henry's tip which had often done Bertie a bit of good:

> Never forget, my boy, that if you stand outside Romano's in the Strand, you can see the clock on the wall of the Law Courts down in Fleet Street. Most people who don't know don't believe it's possible, because there are a couple of churches in the middle of the road, and you would think they would be in the way. But you can, and it's worth knowing. You can win a lot of money betting on it with fellows who haven't found it out.

Miss Tomlinson interrupts him and asks for a little story. He is just embarking on the one about the stockbroker and the chorus girl when Miss Tomlinson cuts him short and calls for the school song, herself 'rising like an iceberg' – a wonderful and typical Wodehousian image. I hope nobody will do a Miss Tomlinson on me tonight.

I have two reasons for being on my feet. The first is Edward Cazalet's power of persuasion. The second is that like everyone else, I have an abiding love of Wodehouse's books. One grows up with them, and one goes on ageing with them while the characters and stories remain ageless. This agelessness, this timeless quality, is part of his secret. The more solemn type of literary critic can be heard complaining that the Wodehouse world remained frozen in 1927 or 1912 or 1932, or some other date on which, significantly, the critics can't agree. But that misses the point. Wodehouse created a world, one entirely his and nobody else's: this is the universal mark of a great and enduring writer. One condition of doing this so completely is that it should obey its creator's laws. Wodehouse lived to a great age; he never stopped writing, and he put time and age to proper use. We are all preoccupied with time and its passing: it is a pretty big subject. Proust, for example, wrote millions of words to recapture time past; Wodehouse required rather fewer words and tackled the problem more manageably. While we enjoy him, we are still young in heart and mind – and so is he. Behind the solemn critic's view lurks a notion that a writer's true function is to describe, to reflect, and to change society, to be realistic and progressive. This doctrine entered Western civilization in the middle years of the nineteenth century as a hangover from Romanticism. It has done a good deal of harm. At best it produces modishness; at worst the enslavement of artists to particular political regimes, some of them abhorrent. Most of the great nineteenth-century writers – Dickens, Flaubert, Turgenev, Tolstoy on his best form – go beyond mere realism; their direct social messages are not the most important things about their works. Wodehouse is in this healthy tradition of a reaction against mere realism. Some might say that his world has gone. To them we reply that his works allow us to recapture it. But I don't believe that his characters have gone: we all know Gussie Fink-Nottle, Bingo Little and Barmy Fotheringay-Phipps, Lord Emsworth and the efficient Baxter, headmasters like the Rev. Aubrey Upjohn, aunts benevolent and aunts much more tricky, girls like Bobbie

Wickham who lead men astray, and bishops who are responsive to the Rev. Augustine Mulliner's excellent tonic 'Buck-U-Uppo'. We know these people, but not because they are minutely described. They are all linked by, and visible to us through a temperament and a style, a style apparently effortless but full of artifice, effervescently conversational, beautiful in its balance and its cadences:

> I don't know if you happen to know what the word excesses means, but these are what Pongo's Uncle Fred from the country, when in London, invariably commits.

Gibbon would have been pleased with that sentence, just as Shakespeare and the contributors to the Bible (and other authors too numerous to mention) must be grateful to Wodehouse for what he has done for them. Their good things have been fruitfully adopted and 're-cycled'. Shakespeare is not just a man who wrote cosmically important plays performed in official theatres: he is part of everyone's world through Wodehouse's use of him. Molière and Racine must be gnashing their teeth for want of a French Wodehouse. The young in England read Wodehouse (I have firm evidence on this); they learn that Shakespeare is not just a school text, not just a classic author, but a man with plenty of good tips about life.

I have said nothing about all the other things Wodehouse was in his time: a writer of lyrics who was a major force in the American or Anglo-American musical tradition, film-script author in barmy Hollywood, a truly professional journalist. I can't think of any other writer who has so completely abolished the ocean which divides us from the United States. Politics may occasionally divide: Wodehouse unites. He also unites the writers, a lonely and misunderstood lot, and the public. For it was not critics but fellow-authors, notably Hilaire Belloc and Evelyn Waugh, who first insisted that Wodehouse was a great writer with a permanent place in literature. They were only saying eloquently what the general public already knew – a fact which, despite his modesty, must have considerably pleased Wodehouse and no doubt also amused him. When that Irishman, who should have known better, called him 'the performing flea of English literature',

Wodehouse used the phrase for one of his volumes of reminiscences. I daresay he would have been able to do something with the Victorian author's description of a colleague as 'a louse in the locks of literature'.

I have one final claim to have inflicted these thoughts on you. I belong to Bertie Wooster's college (a point now conclusively established by J. H. C. Morris in *Thank You, Wodehouse* (1981)); and it was the President of Magdalen, George Gordon, who as Vice-Chancellor presented Wodehouse with his honorary degree at Oxford. That was an action by which the University honoured itself, and made up for the accident of the wildly fluctuating rupee which affected the pension of Wodehouse's father and so prevented his son from coming to Oxford.

By this agreeable and festive occasion, linked as it is with a splendid exhibition which owes much to the spirit and generosity of James Heineman, we are paying a tribute to Plum which he would, I think, have approved of. I am certain that he would have felt deeply honoured by Your Majesty's critical discernment. But in loving Wodehouse's works, Your Majesty is only giving one more proof (not that we need one) of how much you share – and have shared all your life – with your devoted subjects.

Angus Macintyre, born 1935, served in the Coldstream Guards and read Modern History at Hertford College, Oxford. He has been, for nineteen years, Official Fellow and Tutor in Modern History and, for two years, Vice-President of Magdalen College, Oxford. He is author of The Liberator: Daniel O' Connell *(1965) and other historical works. He has been Editor of* The English Historical Review *since 1978. He contributed to* Thank You, Wodehouse *(1981) by J. H. C. Morris, also Fellow of Magdalen. Recreations: cricket and bibliomania.*